Praise for *We Found a Ha...*

"The kind of bedtime story that children will return to again and again"
The Irish Times

"A masterpiece of honest feelings, emotional tension and poetic restraint"
The New York Times

"Essential reading for every family"
Daily Mail

"A gem of a book to read, re-read and savour"
Julia Eccleshare's Book of the Month, LoveReading

"The final instalment in Jon Klassen's trilogy doesn't disappoint"
Evening Standard

"A finely observed tale of friendship, sharing and generosity of spirit
… quietly profound and very special"
South Wales Evening Post

"Jon Klassen is still the master of deadpan comedy
and devastating comic timing. An absolute joy"
The Irish Independent

"The ideal story to share with youngsters beginning
to learn the nuances of friendship"
Booktrust

A *New York* ... k of the Year, 2016

For Will and Justin, always

First published 2016 by Walker Books Ltd
87 Vauxhall Walk, London SE11 5HJ

This edition published 2017

2 4 6 8 10 9 7 5 3 1

© 2016 Jon Klassen

The right of Jon Klassen to be identified as the
author and illustrator of this work has been asserted by him
in accordance with the Copyright, Designs and Patents Act 1988

This book has been typeset in New Century Schoolbook

Printed in China

British Library Cataloguing in Publication Data:
a catalogue record for this book is available from the British Library

ISBN 978-1-4063-7382-0

www.walker.co.uk

WE
FOUND
A
HAT

JON KLASSEN

WALKER BOOKS
AND SUBSIDIARIES
LONDON · BOSTON · SYDNEY · AUCKLAND

PART ONE

Finding the Hat

We found a hat.

We found it together.

But there is only one hat.

And there are two of us.

How does it look on me?

It looks good on you.

How does it look on me?

It looks good on you too.

It looks good on both of us.

But it would not be right
if one of us had a hat
and the other did not.

There is only one thing to do.
We must leave the hat here
and forget that we found it.

Watching

the

Sunset

We are watching the sunset.

We are watching it together.

What are you thinking about?

I am thinking about the sunset.

What are you thinking about?

Nothing.

Going

to

Sleep

We are going to sleep.

We are going to sleep here together.

Are you almost asleep?

I am almost asleep.

Are you all the way asleep?

I am all the way asleep.
I am dreaming a dream.

What are you dreaming about?

I will tell you what I am dreaming about.

I am dreaming that
I have a hat.
It looks very good
on me.

You are also there.
You also have a hat.

It looks very good on you too.

We both have hats?

JON KLASSEN is the creator of the much-acclaimed Hat trilogy which includes *I Want My Hat Back*, the Kate Greenaway Medal and Caldecott Medal winner *This Is Not My Hat*, and *We Found a Hat*. He is also the illustrator of *The Wolf, the Duck and the Mouse*, *Triangle* and the two Caldecott Honor books, *Extra Yarn* and *Sam and Dave Dig a Hole*, all written by his friend, author Mac Barnett. Originally from Niagara Falls, Canada, Jon Klassen now lives in Los Angeles, USA.

Find Jon online at burstofbeaden.com
and on Twitter as @burstofbeaden.

Look out for:

978-1-4063-3853-9

978-1-4063-5343-3